For Jazz
~ *J.T.*

LITTLE TIGER PRESS
1 The Coda Centre, 189 Munster Road,
London SW6 6AW
www.littletiger.co.uk

First published in Great Britain 2003
This edition published 2016

Text copyright © Andrew Murray 2003
Illustrations copyright © Jack Tickle 2003
Visit Jack Tickle at wwwChapmanandWarnes.com

ISBN 978-1-84869-456-9
Printed in China
LTP/1900/1573/0616

1 2 3 4 5 6 7 8 9 10

This Little Tiger book belongs to:

_____

_____

_____

The Very Sleepy Sloth

Andrew Murray   Jack Tickle

LITTLE TIGER PRESS
London

Deep in the jungle,
early in the morning,
the sloth was fast asleep.

But the rest of
the animals were
wide awake.

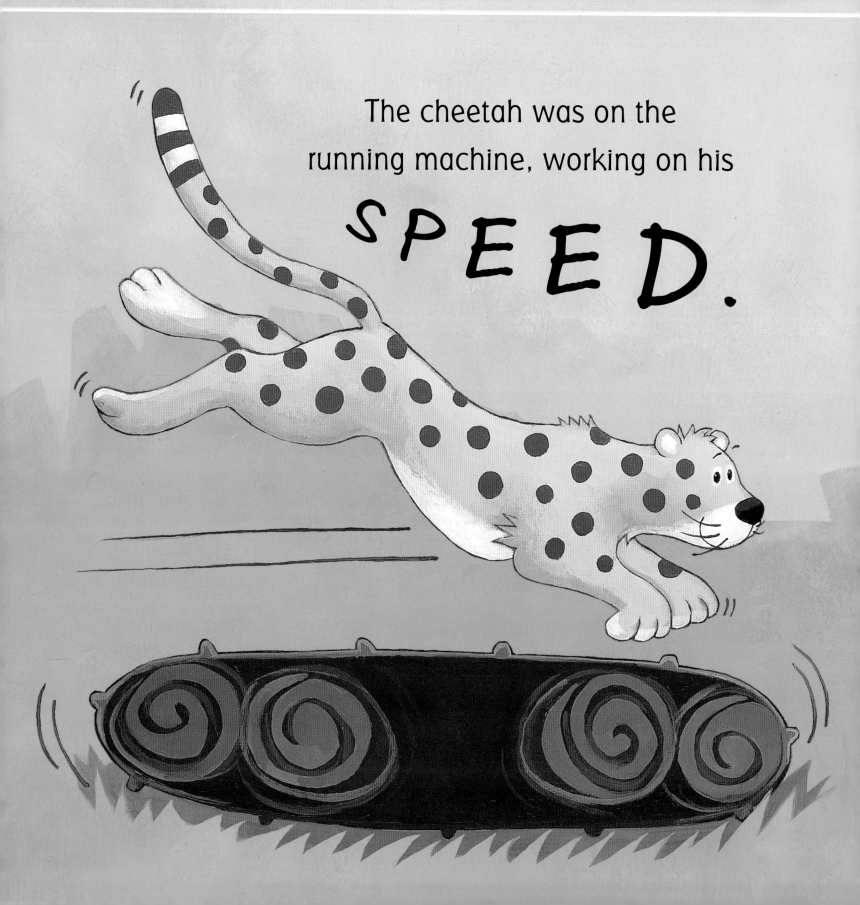

The cheetah was on the running machine, working on his

SPEED.

The elephant was lifting
heavy weights,
working on her

STRENGTH.

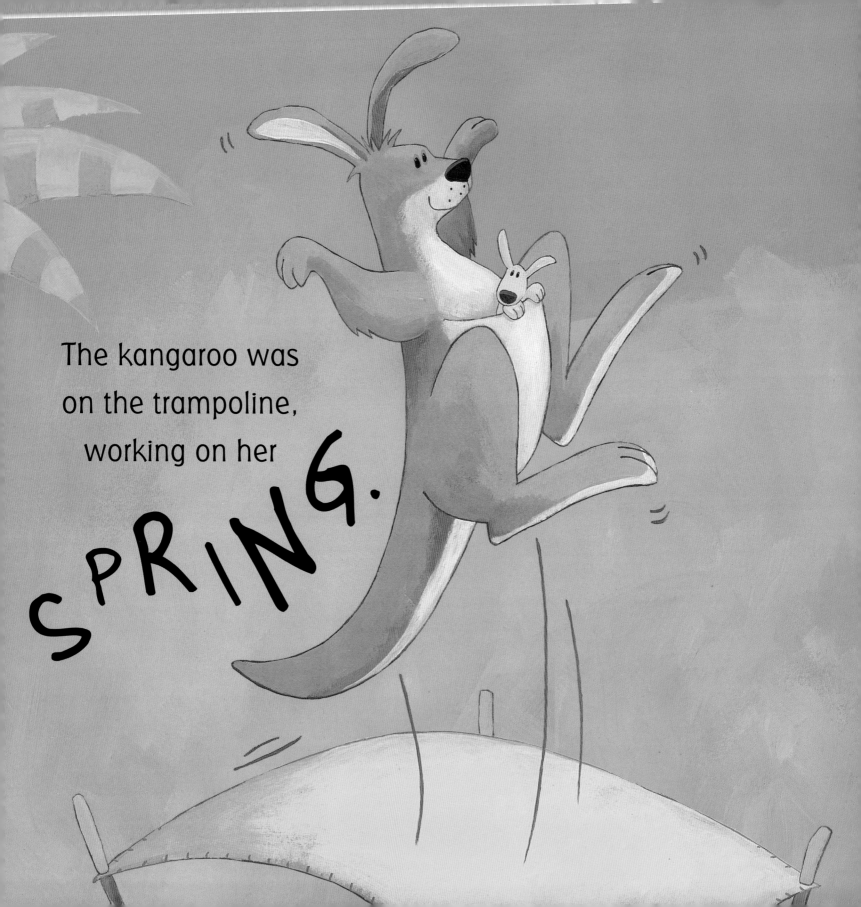

The kangaroo was on the trampoline, working on her SPRING.

The monkey was
on the high bars,
working on his S W I N G.

While the sloth stayed
in his hammock,
working on his sleep.

"That sloth is so lazy,"
said Cheetah.

"All he does is lie there!"
agreed Elephant.

"Just dozing in his hammock,"
added Kangaroo.

"Hey, Sloth!" called Monkey.
"We're all working hard here.
Why don't you get up and
do something?"

Sloth slowly opened one eye.
"Monkey," he said. "If you're
so hard-working, you try
lifting Elephant's weights."

"Easy!" said Monkey,
and he tried to lift
the weights.
Elephant giggled as . . .

oooOOOof!

Monkey toppled right over.

"Elephant!" said Monkey gruffly. "If you think it's so easy, you jump like Kangaroo!"

So Elephant tried to
jump on the trampoline.
Kangaroo tutted as . . .

CRASH!

Elephant fell right through. "Don't tut at me, Kangaroo!" said Elephant grumpily. "Can *you* run like Cheetah?"

So Kangaroo tried the running machine.
Cheetah chuckled as
Kangaroo landed on . . .

her bottom!

OOOOOOW!

"Cheetah!" said Kangaroo crossly. "If you're so clever, you swing like Monkey."

So Cheetah climbed
the high bars and
swung right into . . .

Elephant.

EEE EK!

By now, everyone was very hot,
very tired, and very, very cross.

"This is useless," they muttered.
"Who caused all this trouble?"

"It wasn't me,"
said Cheetah.
"I was busy running."

"It wasn't me,"
said Kangaroo.
"I was busy bouncing."

"It wasn't me," said Elephant.

"I was busy lifting weights."

"And it wasn't me,"
said Monkey.

"I was busy swinging."

All the animals turned
and looked at . . .

SLOTH!

"Hey, Sloth," they called.

"You started this!"

Sloth turned lazily.
"You must see by now,"
he said. "We were all busy doing
what we do best. Even me!"

The animals thought about it.
"Yes!" they cried. "We're all good at
running or jumping or lifting or swinging.
But Sloth is the very best at . . ."

"SNO

OZING!"

"Exactly!" said Sloth.
And with a stretch
and a yawn he fell
fast asleep!